Anne Rockwell

Once Upon a Time This Morning

pictures by
Sucie Stevenson

Greenwillow Books, New York

TABLE OF CONTENTS

THE EARLY BIRD

Once upon a time there was an early bird. It sat on a branch of a tree and began to sing its song before the sun was up. The tree where it sat was right outside a little boy's bedroom window.

The early bird sang and sang until the little boy woke up.

"I'll go get my mother and father," the little boy said to the early bird. "So they can hear you sing, too."

First the little boy woke up his mother. Then he woke up his father.

"Go back to bed," they both said in sleepy voices. "It's much too early to get up."

But the little boy would not go back to bed.

The little boy's father said, "Okay—come on. Back to bed you go!" He picked up his little boy and took him back to his very own bed in his very own room.

But when the little boy's father heard the early bird singing its song, he sat down with the little boy and listened.

As they listened together, the sky turned pink and the sun began to come up. Then lots of birds, all twittering and chirping their own good-morning songs, flew into the little boy's yard to join the early bird in song.

Soon the sky turned blue, and it really was time to get up.

THE LOST BUNNY

Once upon a time there was a bunny who was lost. He wasn't up on the chair or down on the rug. He wasn't under the bed or on top of the bookcase. He wasn't behind the door or beside the basket. He wasn't in the closet or out in the yard. He wasn't here, and he wasn't there.

No, that poor little bunny wasn't anywhere—not anywhere at all—and the little girl who loved him was very sad.

She searched here, and she searched there, but she couldn't find the lost bunny.

Then, after she had searched for a long time, something wonderful happened. Guess what? The bunny was hiding in the toy chest, exactly where he belonged.

Let me tell you—that little girl was very happy indeed! And from that day on her bunny was never lost again.

A LITTLE BOY WHO FORGOT

Once upon a time there was a little boy whose mother had to go to the city on the train.

His baby-sitter came to take him to her house. The little boy could hardly wait, because his baby-sitter had a new puppy.

As soon as the baby-sitter rang the doorbell, the boy ran to her, and they went down the street to her white house on the corner.

The little boy played with the puppy until it was time for the puppy to take a nap. Then the little boy watched the tropical fish swim. He helped his baby-sitter sweep the floor and work in the garden. Before long, it was time for lunch.

As soon as the little boy sat down at the table, he remembered something. "Uh-oh!" he said. "I forgot to kiss my mother good-bye." The little boy began to worry. "I'd better go home and give her a kiss!" he said.

But the little boy's mother was far away in the city, and he couldn't kiss her good-bye.

When the little boy's mother came to get him, he ran to her and said, "Mommy! I forgot to kiss you good-bye this morning!"

"So you did," his mother said as he gave her a very big kiss. She gave him a big kiss, and a hug, too.

Then the little boy and his mother walked home together.

PURPLE AND PURPLE

Once upon a time there was a little girl who liked purple. She didn't like any other colors. Not red, not green, not blue, not yellow, not orange, either; not brown, not black, not white. Only purple.

She had a purple dress and a purple skirt and a purple jacket. She had two purple shirts and one purple turtleneck. She had two pairs of purple tights and a pair of purple striped socks. She even had a pair of purple sneakers, but one day her purple sneakers got too small.

The little girl went to the shoe store with her mother. She tried on brown shoes and red shoes, white shoes, black shoes, and one pair of blue shoes, but none of them were right. Some fit, and some didn't—but none of them were purple.

Finally the salesman found a pair of purple shoes. He put them on the little girl's feet, and they fit just right.

"Good! We'll take them," said the little girl's mother.

"No," whispered the little girl to her mother. "I don't want these shoes. I want those." She pointed to a pair of sneakers in the store window.

The salesman took them out of the window and tried them on the little girl's feet. They fit just right.

"I want these," the little girl said.

"But they're not purple," her mother said.

"I know," said the little girl. "Now I like pink."

The little girl was very proud of her brand-new pink sneakers. They were just as beautiful as they could be.

MINE!

Once upon a time there was a little boy who always said "Mine!" in a very loud voice. He said it about his own toys, and he said it about other children's toys, too.

One day he came to play with another little boy, who was very polite and always shared his toys.

"Mine!" said the first little boy as he grabbed a beautiful, shiny, red fire engine.

The second little boy didn't say anything.

"Mine!" said the first little boy as he grabbed a teddy bear.

The second little boy didn't say anything.

"Mine! Mine! Mine!" the first little boy said all morning, again and again—until it was snack time.

There were two chocolate-chip cookies on a plate on the kitchen table and two glasses of milk.

"Mine!" said the first little boy. He grabbed both cookies, which was certainly not at all polite.

By now the second little boy had had enough. "No, it's not yours! That cookie is mine!" he said in a very loud voice. He took his cookie away from the little boy who always said "Mine!" and ate it all up, every last crumb.

The first little boy was so surprised that he just ate his cookie and drank his milk. He didn't say a word.

After that the two little boys always played together very nicely and very politely, and neither one ever said "Mine! Mine! Mine!" again.

THE HAPPY SONG

Once upon a time there was a little girl who was so happy she made up a song. It went like this: "I am so happy! I am so happy! I am very happy today!"

The little girl sang the happy song while she got dressed. She sang it while she brushed her teeth. She sang it while she ate her breakfast and while she rode her tricycle. When she got into her car seat and her mother drove the car down the street to the gas station, she sang the happy song to the people there.

Next she sang the happy song to the people in the post office, and she sang it very loudly indeed to all the people in the supermarket.

The little girl sang the happy song while she ate her lunch. When it was time to take her nap, she sang the happy song very, very softly to her doll and her fuzzy penguin. She sang it so nicely that the doll and the fuzzy penguin soon went to sleep.

And she did, too.

A VERY GOOD SMELL

Once upon a time there was a little boy whose cousin came to visit. She and the little boy played outside in the yard until suddenly they smelled a very good smell.

What do you suppose it was?

It wasn't the purple lilacs blooming on the bush, and it wasn't the green, green grass. It wasn't the little boy's mother's perfume or his father's after-shave. It wasn't the bubble bath or the little boy's rubber ball. It wasn't the pine needles on the tall, tall tree, either. The little boy and his cousin didn't know what it was.

They went to the kitchen. "We smell something good," they said.

"And what do you suppose it is?" the little boy's mother said.

"We don't know," they answered.

"Well, then, I'll show you," said the little boy's mother.

She took a pot holder, opened the oven door, and pulled out a very hot cookie sheet. And on that very hot cookie sheet was a big, brown gingerbread man with raisin buttons and eyes.

As soon as the gingerbread man had cooled off a bit, the little boy and his cousin helped make him a sugar-frosting face with a wide, smiling mouth and swirls of white, curly hair.

That gingerbread man certainly was beautiful. He looked every bit as good as he smelled. The cousins looked at him and admired him for a long, long time.

But that afternoon they discovered the gingerbread man was delicious, too.

THE BUSY FATHER

Once upon a time there was a father who was terribly busy. He was much too busy to play with his little boy.

The little boy's father had to bundle the newspapers for recycling. He had to fix the broken curtain rod. He had to hang a picture. He had to paint the old porch chair, and he had to write a letter.

The little boy wanted to help, but his father said he couldn't. The little boy didn't know how to tie a knot; he was too little to climb the ladder or hammer a nail. And he certainly was much, much too little to paint with smelly, sticky green paint or write with a pen full of black ink.

So the little boy had to wait. He waited and waited, and waited some more. He was quite patient.

Finally the little boy's father wasn't busy anymore. He had time to play.

He and his little boy sat on the floor and built a beautiful tall tower of blocks that didn't fall down for hours. Not until it was time for supper.

THE LITTLE GIRL
WHO DIDN'T WANT A BATH

Once upon a time there was a little girl who didn't want to take a bath.

"Look," said her mother. "Your duck is taking a bath."

"But I don't want to," said the little girl.

"Now the fish is taking a bath," said her mother.

"I still don't want to," said the little girl.

"The beautiful mermaid says this is a very nice bubble bath," said her mother.

"No, it's not," said the little girl. "And I don't want a bath."

Soon the little red sailboat was taking a bath, and the scuba diver was taking a bath, too. But the little girl still would not take a bath.

Then the great big whale got in the tub full of bubble bath. That great big whale had such a happy smile that the little girl decided she wanted to take a bath, too.

So she did. She took a bath for a long, long time. She splashed in the water with the duck and the fish, the beautiful mermaid and the little red sailboat, the scuba diver, and the great big smiling whale. Before you knew it—they were all nice and clean.

THE BIGGEST MOON

Once upon a time there was a little boy who wouldn't go to sleep because he couldn't.

He had warm pajamas with feet. He had a white bed with a cozy blue blanket. He had a soft pillow and a cuddly bear to sleep next to him. He had a mother and father to kiss him good-night and read him stories, but still he wouldn't—he couldn't—go to sleep.

His mother turned out the light and sat on his bed and sang him a lullaby in the darkness. It was a very nice lullaby, but he wouldn't go to sleep.

"Where is it?" he asked. "Where did it go?"

"Where did what go?" his father asked.

"The moon. The biggest moon I ever saw," said the little boy.

His mother and father looked out the window, but they couldn't see any moon.

Then all of a sudden the moon rose up from behind a dark tree. It was very big and very bright and very round.

"There it is!" said the little boy. "The biggest moon I ever saw!"

He held his bear up so he could see the big, bright, round moon, too.

Then the little boy put his head down on his pillow, hugged his cuddly bear, and closed his eyes.

His mother gave him a kiss. His father did, too. Then they tiptoed out of the room, for now their little boy was fast asleep.

And while he slept, the biggest, brightest, roundest, most beautiful moon he had ever seen shone outside in the sky all night long.

for Snowy
—A. R.

for Jack Stevenson
—S. S.

Acrylics and permanent black ink were used for the
full-color art. The text type is Cheltenham ITC.

Printed in Singapore by Tien Wah Press
First Edition   10 9 8 7 6 5 4 3 2 1

Library of Congress Cataloging-in-Publication Data

Rockwell, Anne F.
Once upon a time this morning / by Anne Rockwell ;
pictures by Suçie Stevenson.
       p.   cm.
Summary: A series of stories about different aspects
of a child's daily life, illustrating various types of behavior.
ISBN 0-688-14706-2 (trade)
ISBN 0-688-14707-0 (lib. bdg.)
1. Children's stories, American.
[1. Behavior—Fiction.   2. Short stories.]
I. Stevenson, Suçie, ill.   II. Title.
PZ7.R5943Oq   1997   [E]—dc20
96-6349   CIP   AC